for my father
Nat J. Silverstein
(1905 – 1969)
much beloved

. . .and for the people of this planet,
that we may feel more beloved
in each other's presence
sharing the gift of life
together

"Every once in a while someone comes along
and creates a jewel which is full of lustre.
This particular jewel shows and tells, in a
very simple way, what a miracle a human being
is and how really beautiful life can be."
— Virginia Satir

"'Life Is A Gift' captures the
excitement and simplicity of
moments when we awaken to life.
It's about the secret
that isn't a secret."
— Marilyn Ferguson

Publisher's ISBN: 0-9609888-0-7

Printed in the United States of America

Twelfth printing

Published by Red Rose Press
3467 Red Rose Drive
Encino, CA 91436

15	14	13	12
97	96	95	94

Life Is a Gift

wordscapes
by
Rusty Berkus

illustrations by
Christa Wollan

Red Rose Press

The Gift is there
You need only see it, to have it

Life is a party
to which you have been invited
Are you going to sit
on the sidelines
Or join in the dance?

You are not a
xerox
of anyone else
Each Life is an
original work of art
When are you going to start
signing autographs?

Life feels a lot lighter
when we are aware
that it is a grand
experiment;
for the Universe is a laboratory
where there are
no mistakes —
only different outcomes

Life incites you
        to run from the Truth
        the whole Truth
        and nothing but the Truth
                If you care to.

Life invites you
   to live by the Truth
   the whole Truth
   and nothing but the Truth
      If you dare to.

the big Lie about Life
is that there is something to
fear
      the big Truth about Life
      is that fear is an
      illusion
            Let's get hooked on the big
            Truth.

Life allows you to be the
writer,
director,
choreographer,
editor
and Star
of your own scenario —
and you don't have to sleep with the producer
to get the job.

Life is a classroom
    where it's okay to ask questions,
        and if you don't get all the answers
        you
            pass
                anyway.

Calling all children
hiding out in their grown-up bodies
who long to be
joyful, funful,
freeful
come out, come out, wherever you are
and play in the now-sun
of your
Life

The great big Secret about
Life
is that there is no secret

How
lovely
to know
that you
don't have to
be perfect —
all
you need do
is to
be.

Life
is
so
simple
that
we
have
managed
to
make
an
outrageous
complexity
of
it

Life's most painful losses
can
lead
to
Life's
most
beautiful
findings.

Life
is
full of
remissions,
reprieves,
resurrections
and
rebirths

the beauty of one's Life
can only be measured
by the quality of
Love
in
it

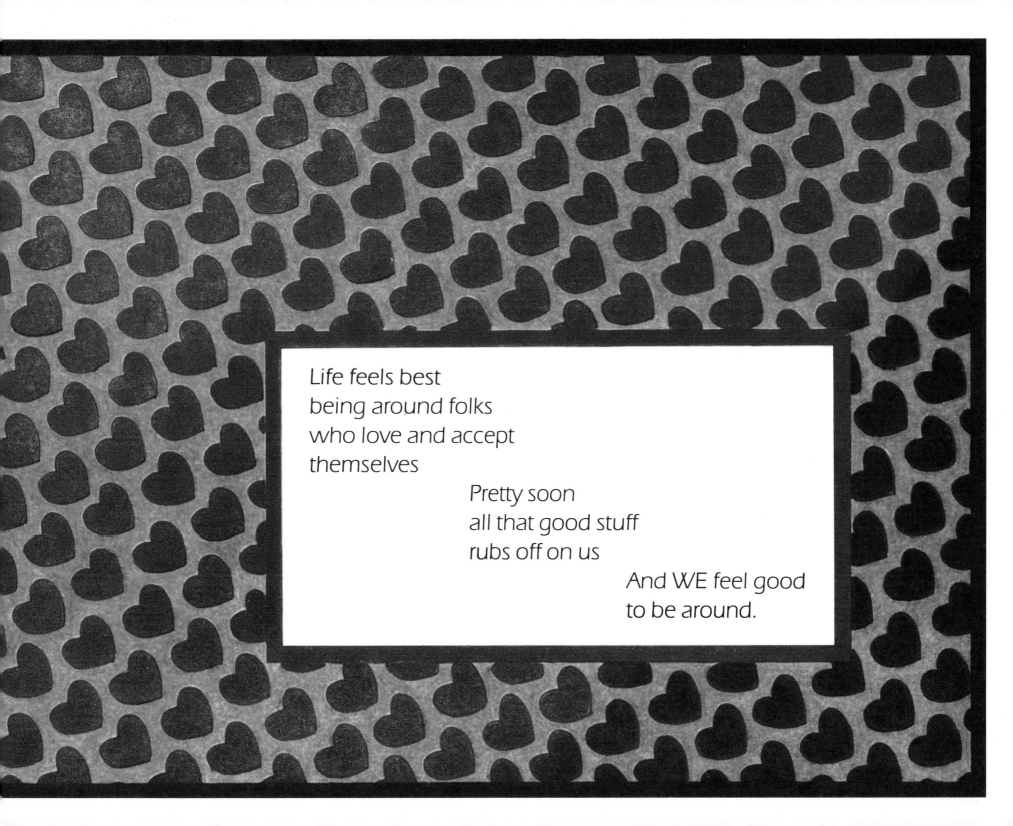

Life feels best
being around folks
who love and accept
themselves

Pretty soon
all that good stuff
rubs off on us

And WE feel good
to be around.

Life moves moment to moment,

miracle to miracle

There comes
that mysterious meeting in Life,
when someone acknowledges
who we are and what we can be,
igniting the circuits of our highest
potential

I see this
as the appearance of an angel,
and know it to be a moment of
Grace.

Question: how can you tell the guru in the black robe
from the guru in the white robe?
Answer: the guru in the black robe
keeps you wondering
whether it is safe for you to go off into the sunset
without him.
the guru in the white robe
smiles serenely
as you bid each other farewell,
having taught you to become
your own guru.

Life has lustre when we discover
our jewelness
and display all the facets of
our being

Life can be seen as
a celebration
a challenge
a journey
and much more —

The Gift is there
You need only see it, to have it

About the Author

Rusty Berkus is a poet, composer,
lyricist and has her Masters Degree in
Marriage and Family Counseling. She is also the
author of the inspirational works, "Appearances",
"To Heal Again", "Soulprints", "Nell the Nebbish",
"In Celebration of Friendship" and
"The Consiousness of Deserving".

From her personal life experience,
Rusty has found that we are all healers
and teachers for each other. Using poetry and
other therapeutic modalities, she has discovered that
the most powerful energy which binds our wounds
and renders us whole is love.

About the Artist

Christa Wollan is a graphic designer.
She is also the illustrator of "Appearances",
"To Heal Again", and "Soulprints".

Christa believes that we are all
artists, creating the world around us through
the medium of our lives. To experience the positive
change we desire, we need only to extend the
power of our love, light, truth and joy
through all that we say and do.

Acknowledgements
I wish to express my deepest gratitude to all the
loving people in my life who like mystical midwives
contributed their valuable time, energy, expertise
and support enabling me to give birth to this book.

With heartfelt love and deep appreciation
to the following Patron Sponsors
who so generously contributed
to the printing of this book:

Cami Berkus
Steven Berkus
Laura G. Bramlette
Linda & Peter Bren
Adrienne Brookstone
Rita Cooper
Dorothy Frueh
Dr. Sandra S. Grifman
David L. Harris
Hank Harmon
Al H. Jacobson
Venu Katz
Susan & Bernard Kamins
David Kelton
Suzanne Lawrence
Deanna Lococo
Paula & J.J. Lynch Jr.
Ruth Merin
Erlend Peterson
Scott Sevel
Elizabeth R. V. Welborn
David Williams
Tatiana Wrenfeather

A MESSAGE FROM
RED ROSE PRESS

One of the finest gifts you can give to another
is to inspire and enhance that person's life
with a greater sense of self-acceptance,
dignity, joy and inner peace.

In the simple act of giving a gift
of any one of these beautiful books,
you have greatly contributed
to the well-being of another.
In the simple act of receiving the gift
of one of these fine books,
the reader is given the rare opportunity
to awaken to his or her own inherent greatness.

Red Rose Press is proud to have made
a unique contribution to the world of publishing
and gift-giving by bringing uplifting
and profoundly healing messages
to hundreds of thousands of people
of all ages and in all walks of life.

Just as the unfolding of a rose is invisible to the eye
when it comes to full bloom,
thus the depth and value of these books
bring their subtle treasures to each person
according to their own unique needs for growth.

RED ROSE PRESS
1-800-789-ROSE

Thank you for purchasing a Red Rose Press book. We take great pride in publishing high quality gift books specializing in inspirational, therapeutic/alternative healing and self-esteem subjects for children and adults.

If you would like to know more about our books, please complete this self-addressed card and mail it to us. We will be happy to send you a catalog.

Name _____

Address _____

City _____

State/Zip _____

IMPORTANT: *Please answer the following:*

How did you first find out about Red Rose Press' books?
_____

Name of book(s) & where purchased.
_____

Occupation:
_____

Male ❑   Female ❑   Age: _____

Comments:
_____
_____

RED ROSE PRESS
3467 RED ROSE DRIVE
ENCINO, CA 91436

PLEASE
PLACE
STAMP
HERE